It's Okay,
I Toot Too!

PAGE PUBLISHING
Conneaut Lake, PA

First originally published by Page Publishing 2023

ISBN 979-8-88793-514-0 (hc)
ISBN 979-8-88793-504-1 (digital)

Printed in the United States of America

It's Okay, I Toot Too!

Eileen Tanaka-Sylvia

Eileen Tanaka-Sylvia

The flowers are wilted

The dog ran away

Why, oh why

did I eat beans today?

My body digests the
foods I like to eat

The smells that come out
are not too sweet

I tell my sisters to run and hide

There are gurgly noises
rumbling inside

Chocolate, cabbage,

and mostly beans

A squeaker, a blaster

You know what that means

Girls say they peep…

Moms don't at all

We all make a blast

When we hear nature call.

Pull my finger
my dear old friend
But I do warn you
that it may be the *end*

Run for the hills,
hide under your bed
If you stick around
You will be dead

God made our bodies

Each a perfect one

He threw in the toots

To make life fun

Sometimes they're smelly

Sometimes they're loud

When people say, "Oh Robby,"

I say, "'scuse me. I did
it and I'm proud!"

About the Author

Born and raised in the San Francisco Bay Area, Eileen was encouraged by her parents to be creative. Learning crafts and skills from her talented parents and several aunties, Eileen became a successful tailor in her own shop, Said with Threads.

Whether the material was of wood, fabric, clay, or glass, Eileen enjoyed cutting the material apart then reconstructing the pieces back into something new.

While raising children, Mandy, Ashley, Rob, and grandson Adam with husband Robert, Eileen found many stories inspired by the pieces of the childhood lives the kids left behind. These stories would be destined to be put together into books to be shared with everyone.

Printed in the USA
CPSIA information can be obtained
at www.ICGtesting.com
JSHW070205040124
54581JS00016B/3

9 798887 935140